ALECA*ZAMM
Fools Them All

Read more about Aleca's adventures:

Aleca Zamm Is a Wonder

Aleca Zamm Is Ahead of Her Time

ALECA*ZAMM
Fools Them All

GINGER RUE

Aladdin

NEW YORK   LONDON   TORONTO   SYDNEY   NEW DELHI

ALADDIN

An imprint of Simon & Schuster Children's Publishing Division
1230 Avenue of the Americas, New York, New York 10020
First Aladdin hardcover edition January 2018
Text copyright © 2018 by Ginger Stewart
Cover illustrations copyright © 2018 by Zoe Persico
Also available in an Aladdin paperback edition.
All rights reserved, including the right of reproduction in whole or in part in any form.
ALADDIN and related logo are registered trademarks of Simon & Schuster, Inc.
For information about special discounts for bulk purchases, please contact
Simon & Schuster Special Sales at 1-866-506-1949 or business@simonandschuster.com.
The Simon & Schuster Speakers Bureau can bring authors to your live event. For more information or to book an event contact the Simon & Schuster Speakers Bureau at 1-866-248-3049 or visit our website at www.simonspeakers.com.
Jacket designed by Karin Paprocki
Interior designed by Hilary Zarycky
The text of this book was set in ITC New Baskerville.
Manufactured in the United States of America 1217 FFG
2 4 6 8 10 9 7 5 3 1
Library of Congress Control Number 2017940733
ISBN 978-1-4814-7067-4 (hc)
ISBN 978-1-4814-7066-7 (pbk)
ISBN 978-1-4814-7068-1 (eBook)

For Mother

CONTENTS

1

Ford Kimble Knows Almost Everything / 1

2

Guess What Ford Can Do / 15

3

We'll Cross That Bridge When We Come to It (I Hope) / 20

4

I Wish I Could've Enjoyed That Burn Longer / 27

5

I Don't Think So Great under Pressure / 34

6

Of All the Celebrities in the World, I Pick This One / 39

7

Brett Lasseter Is Going to Get His One Day, but I Can't
Wait That Long / 48

8

It's Not Stealing If It's for a Good Cause / 57

9

The Most Majestic Bridge I Never Saw / 63

10

Number One Fan / 70

11
I'm Pretty Sure Everyone Secretly Still Likes the
Whoop-Dee-Doos / 75

12
Aunt Zephyr's Wonky Wonder-ing / 86

13
Someone Is on Our Roof, and It Isn't Santa / 93

14
I've Never Been This Excited about Research
in My Whole Life / 102

15
"Walking on Air" Isn't Just an Expression / 110

16
A Short Walk on a Long Bridge / 115

17
Saving Aunt Zephyr from the Soaps / 121

ALECA*ZAMM
Fools Them All

Ford Kimble Knows
Almost Everything

It was early Tuesday morning, a good twenty minutes before the first bell. That is just way too early to be at school, especially when you don't want to be there anyway. But my reason for being early was that Ford Kimble was supposed to show up at any minute.

At least I hoped so.

I sat on the third swing from the left—my lucky swing—on the school playground. The reason it is my lucky swing is because one time in first grade a mean girl pushed me off it so that she could have it. And then, when she tried to get on, she missed and lost her balance and fell right onto her booty. If that is not a lucky swing, then I don't know what is!

Anyway, back to Ford.

I'd slipped a note into his desk the morning before. It told him to meet me here so we could talk about what had happened at my birthday party last Friday night, when I'd stopped time at the skating rink and Ford hadn't frozen along with everyone else. It's this thing I can do just by speaking my name. I just say, "Aleca Zamm!" and then it's like everything turns into a photograph—everything stops happening. Well, except for me. And except for Aunt Zephyr. And also except for Ford Kimble, apparently, which was how Aunt Zephyr and I had realized that we weren't the only ones, that Ford Kimble must be a Wonder too. Now all I needed to do was find out what Ford knew.

I wasn't sure, though, how much help Ford would be. He was way smart, but from the small amount of time I'd spent with him at the skating rink, he seemed like he would rather talk about how machinery works or about math facts. And let's just say that math facts aren't exactly my specialty. So I was worried that Ford and I wouldn't have a lot in common. But Aunt Zephyr had told me that just because someone is wired differently from how you are doesn't mean that they are wired wrong. And if anybody ought to believe that, it's us Wonders.

Besides, I had to try to talk to Ford. Chances

were that he knew a lot about Wonders, just like he knew a lot about nearly everything else. After all, he was the only kid I had ever heard of who'd skipped two grades at once, which is pretty impressive. (I get really proud of myself just for skipping two checkers at once, and grades in school are way harder to skip than checkers.) Ford was only seven and already in the third grade. Also he was the only person I knew of who had become a Wonder before the age of ten. Everyone in my family who'd ever been a Wonder hadn't started Wonder-ing until they were ten, just like me. Aunt Zephyr suggested that Ford might be an extra special Wonder just like he was an extra special smarty-pants. And I wanted to know what he knew.

"Artzy Sneakers," a voice muttered behind

me. "With patented comfort design, Artzy is tops in durability and fashion."

That was another thing Ford liked to do—recite commercials. He had a memory where he could hear something once and then say it exactly the same, word for word. He'd told us about it at the skating rink.

"Ford, you made it!" I said. "Did your parents mind bringing you early?"

"Parents of seven-year-old boys ask lots of questions," Ford said. "Also I don't like this. I had to get up at 6:05 instead of 6:28, and I did not have time to read this morning. But my parents were glad that I have a new friend, so they said I should deviate today."

"Does 'deviate' mean the same thing as 'throw caution to the wind'?" I asked.

"I'm not sure," Ford told me.

"Well, I'm just glad you're here," I added. "Grab a swing." Ford took the swing to the right of mine. He was so small that his feet didn't touch the ground.

Then Ford offered this information: "Continuous centripetal force and acceleration."

"What?"

"In accordance with Newton's first law of motion," he announced, "that is how swings work."

"Okay," I replied. "Let's get down to business. The first day I stopped time, at school on my tenth birthday"—I reminded him of the date—"you saw everything stop, but you didn't stop?"

"Correct," Ford said. "Everything became still and quiet."

"Then you must be a Wonder," I explained. "Because if you weren't, you would have been frozen when time stopped, just like everybody else. Only Wonders are immune to other Wonders. Aunt Zephyr said so. Did you notice anything unusual? I mean, other than time being stopped?"

"No," said Ford.

"It was pretty cool, though, right?" I asked. "Did you see Wendell the Hamster in the first-grade classroom? He was running in midair on his wheel!"

"No," mumbled Ford. He was looking at the ground, not at me, while he spoke. "I crawled into the coat cubby and held my smooth stone. I stayed in the cubby until I heard noise again." He started digging into his pocket. "Have I showed you my smooth stone? You can even hold it if you want to."

"No, thanks, Ford," I answered. "Listen, do you mean to tell me that time stopped and all you did about it was hide in the coat cubby?" I couldn't believe it. That was the last thing I would have done. "Didn't you even take the opportunity to . . . I don't know . . . cheat on a test or something?"

"I don't have to cheat on tests," Ford said. "Tests are easy."

"Right," I replied. "For you, maybe. But didn't you, like, I don't know . . . pour glue into a mean kid's hair or put a bug into a bully's mouth? Because that would be perfectly understandable and I wouldn't, like, judge you for it or anything." I decided not to mention that those were things I had done.

"I like to hold my smooth stone when

my routine changes," Ford insisted. "It feels soothing."

"Oh, okay," I said. Then I shifted in my swing, because all of a sudden I felt kind of uncomfortable, like maybe the pranks I had pulled while time had been stopped hadn't been something anybody else would do.

"But the next day, when I stopped time again in the lunchroom, you must have done some exploring. That's how you saw me."

Ford wasn't looking at me. He was staring into a tree. "Did you know that birds are marvels of engineering?" he asked. "Even if you and I had wings, we could not fly like birds do. We are not properly engineered for it."

"That's very interesting," I assured him. "But what else do you know about Wonders?"

"I know lots of things." Ford almost laughed. "But not about that."

I was getting impatient. "Come on, Ford. You know all about what I can do, but what about you? You must have some Wonder ability, or you would be frozen like everyone else when I stop time. So what's your thing? What can you do?"

"I don't know," began Ford. "It's . . . hazy."

"How do you mean?"

"I'm not entirely sure I can actually *do* anything," he replied. "I have a funny thing, but only when *you* stop time. Not on my own."

"What do you mean, a funny thing? Funny like ha-ha funny, or funny like what's-that-weird-smell funny?"

"Not ha-ha. And not smells," he answered. "I see things."

"What things?"

"Oh, all sorts of things. But all jumbled up."

I was becoming kind of frustrated, because getting the answers I needed was like trying to pull three-year-old smooshed bubble gum out of your soccer cleats. "Like what?"

"I didn't see very much the first time. Probably because I was hiding in the coat cubby because I felt scared."

"The first time?" I asked. "You mean it never happened before the first time I stopped time?"

"Never before."

"And never after?"

"Only when you stop time," he said. "Never on my own."

Wowee, that was interesting. I couldn't wait to tell Aunt Zephyr about it. "Hmmm. So what was your funny thing? What did you do?"

"I saw a desk next to Walter Greenley. It wasn't like the desks we have now. It was an old-fashioned desk, smaller. Wood and cast iron. I didn't try to touch it, but I saw it. Then, when I came out of the coat cubby, the desk was gone. I asked Walter about it, but he told me I was a weirdo. Walter always says that about me."

I didn't know Walter Greenley, but it sounded like he needed a time-out. Anyway, I tried to focus on Ford and what he could do. Seeing an old desk didn't sound like much of a power. "Did you see anything else?"

"Yes," he whispered. "The other times

when you stopped time, there were people who looked . . . different."

"Different how?"

"Do you know my teacher, Mrs. Young?"

"Old Mrs. Young? Sure." Everyone knew old Mrs. Young. She was older than most people's grandmas and had been teaching at our school since some of our parents had been students there.

"Well, once, when time was stopped, I looked at Mrs. Young. There was a woman standing beside her. A young woman. And quite beautiful. Her hair was in a funny style, all curled under at the ends and tall on top. And that made me think, 'Try Emerge Skin Care and watch a younger you emerge overnight. Visit our website to learn how you too can start looking younger today!'"

I ignored the advertisement and focused on the information. "So you're telling me that you saw an oddly dressed stranger next to old Mrs. Young?"

"Oh, no," argued Ford. "Not at all. It *was* Mrs. Young. But not old Mrs. Young. This was young Mrs. Young."

✳ 2 ✳

Guess What Ford Can Do

Ford pulled a small notebook out of his pocket. Now maybe we were getting somewhere!

"This is the woman I saw," he revealed, holding out a copy of a photograph. "I copied this from an old school yearbook in the library. This is Mrs. Young in her first year of teaching here. And that is the woman I saw in my classroom."

"That doesn't make any sense," I said.

Ford told me, "There's more."

"Okay," I replied. "Go on. What else have you seen? Did you see anything the night of my party?"

"Oh yes," he insisted. "I saw the deejay. Next to the deejay. Except the real deejay is twenty-two years old. I know this because I looked at his driver's license when you stopped time. I needed to know his age because there was another deejay standing next to him. But this deejay was not twenty-two. This deejay was my dad's age. He had a potbelly and a large bald spot."

I gasped. "Ford, are you trying to tell me that you see the past and the future?"

Ford sighed. "No. I wouldn't say I've seen either the past or the future entirely. I see only parts of the past and future, and only when you've stopped time. And whatever I see, it's all out of context. And I can't control what I see. Everything is all jumbled up."

"How strange," I declared. I could hardly wrap my brain around it. Of all the possible abilities to have, why *this*? What in the world would anyone be able to do with it? And why would his ability be tied to mine? "I'll have to report all this to Aunt Zephyr immediately."

"Yes," Ford replied. The bird he had been watching in the tree was now sitting on a power line. "We can't do that, either," he pondered. "Sit on wires, I mean."

"Because of the engineering," I confirmed.

"Yes."

I looked at the bird for a minute. Then I exclaimed, "Man, oh, man! You sure have an interesting Wonder ability! I thought stopping time was odd, or teleporting. But this takes the cake! This is even stranger than talking to animals or reading people's minds."

"You can do all that too?" Ford asked. Then I had to tell him about how Aunt Zephyr could teleport and about how my grandpa could talk to animals and about how my great-uncle Zander could read minds. Ford was pretty impressed. "Is everyone in your family a Wonder?" he asked.

"No," I told him. "My sister and parents are Duds. Aunt Zephyr says it can't be helped." Then I had to explain to him what a Dud was. "A Dud is a regular person who isn't a Wonder. It isn't an insult; it's just a fact. Aunt Zephyr says they just don't have the spark."

"Having a spark is kind of fun except when it isn't," Ford said. I knew exactly what he meant. He meant that it's neat to be special but it's sad that other people don't understand. Like how I couldn't tell my cool time-stopping secret to anyone, including my bestie, Maria.

"Well, is that everything?" I inquired. "Is there anything you haven't told me about?"

"There is one thing," he said. "I saw it that day when you were in the lunchroom." Ford shuddered. "It was . . . unnerving."

✳ 3 ✳

We'll Cross That Bridge When We Come to It (I Hope)

"Come on, spill it," I insisted. "What did you see while I was in the lunchroom?"

"As you know, I was walking around outside," Ford replied. "I was hoping to catch a glimpse of whoever or whatever was responsible for what was happening. Or 'not happening' maybe is the better way to say it. I looked in the lunchroom window and saw what you were doing, but then I saw you see me. So I ran away. I ran around to the back of the school, and there it was."

"What?" I could only imagine what Ford must have seen. If he saw things out of their proper time, it could have been something from the past, like a T. rex . . . or something from the future, like a spaceship!

"The bridge," Ford answered.

"Bridge?" I asked. What was so exciting about a bridge? I see bridges all the time. I've even walked or driven over a bunch of them.

"Yes," Ford told me. "It was beautiful. A suspension bridge with trusses." I guess I looked confused, because Ford showed me a picture he'd drawn in his notebook. It was a really pretty bridge, and I had to hand it to him, he was a good artist.

"Where is it, again? I've never seen it before."

"Neither had I," Ford assured me. "And I've never seen it since."

"Wait," I started. "You're telling me that when time stopped, you saw a bridge that isn't there anymore, that disappeared when time started again?"

"Exactly," Ford replied.

I sat thinking for a moment. Then I started swinging. I figured swinging might help me think better, but even a good swing doesn't explain something like that.

"It just doesn't make any sense," I responded.

"Like stopping time," Ford said. "Or teleporting."

"Or talking to animals or reading minds," I agreed. "I see what you mean."

"It was a marvelous bridge," Ford said. "I wish you could've seen it."

"Where did it lead to?" I asked.

Ford laughed. "How should I know?"

"What do you mean? Didn't you walk across it?"

"Walk across it?" Ford repeated.

"You mean you didn't even explore it?"

Ford replied, "I'm seven. I can't even cross the street without holding my mother's hand. And you're suggesting I should have walked across a bridge that suddenly appeared out of nowhere?"

"Duh!" I exclaimed. "If I saw a bridge appear out of nowhere, the first thing I would do is walk across it. Who wouldn't?"

"Someone with common sense," Ford replied.

"Someone who's a big chicken," I said. Though I shouldn't have. I guess because Ford had made a crack, I thought I could make one back. I'd forgotten for a second that he was only seven.

"I am not a chicken!" argued Ford. His eyes started to water. *Oh, great, Aleca,* I thought. *You've made the little Wonder cry!*

"I'm sorry, Ford," I consoled him. "I didn't mean any harm."

"It's not nice to call names," Ford said, sniffing. "It damages the emotions."

"I said I was sorry," I begged. "I wouldn't damage your emotions on purpose."

"I forgive you," Ford mumbled. He

stopped sniffling immediately, like it had all happened a long time ago.

"Thanks," I replied. "But next time if you see a bridge, I think you should cross it. That's what bridges are *for*."

Ford looked at me and squinched his face up.

"What's the matter?" I asked. "Why're you looking at me all funny?"

"I'm studying you," Ford said. "I'm trying to decide if you're really brave or if you just have poor judgment."

"How about this?" I proposed. "Next time you see a bridge, I'll cross it with you. You can hold my hand."

Ford thought about that for a minute. "Maybe," he answered. "But I doubt I'll be seeing any more bridges anyway."

"Why's that?"

"Because I don't see things like that unless you've stopped time. And you're not supposed to stop time."

I had forgotten about that. Aunt Zephyr had forbidden me to stop time anymore. She said I might get caught. We didn't know how many other Wonders there were or if they were all nice. And we didn't know if some Duds were immune to Wonder-ing. It was possible, she'd said, that I might be detected and get into some kind of trouble.

"Oh yeah," I said. "You're right."

I'd sure hate to miss out on crossing that bridge, though.

❋ 4 ❋

I Wish I Could've Enjoyed That Burn Longer

Ford and I walked into school together when the buses began arriving and the car-pool lane was at its busiest. Of course we walked through the front doors just in time to see Madison and Jordan standing around with the other soccer girls.

"Are you babysitting, Aleca?" Madison taunted.

"I think he's her boyfriend," Jordan chimed in. They all giggled.

See, I'm never good at thinking of comebacks until the chance to say them is already gone. If I could've stopped time and thought about it, I might have said something that would've burned them really good. Like maybe, *He's not* my *boyfriend. He's your mom's boyfriend.* (That doesn't actually make any sense, but when you drag somebody's mom or dad into an argument, it always ups the stakes.) Or maybe, *Ford could give you some maturity lessons,* which would have made more sense. But of course I was too pressed for time to say anything good, and I couldn't stop time just to think up an insult. Aunt Zephyr definitely would not have approved.

Madison leaned down and spoke to Ford

in a baby-talk voice. "Didn't your mommy teach you not to play with freaks?"

"Yes," stated Ford, "which is why I won't be playing with you after school, so stop texting me."

Zing! Wow, he totally roasted her! I didn't think Ford could do that!

Even Jordan and the soccer girls laughed. That is, until Madison turned around and gave them the stink eye.

Ford and I walked away before Madison could say anything else. "Hey, that was a good burn!" I told him. "How'd you think of it so fast?"

"I get teased a lot," he replied. "I have memorized twenty-seven comebacks that can easily be modified to different situations."

"Aleca, there you are!" Maria rushed over to me. "Where have you been?"

"What do you mean? I'm here on time," I corrected her.

"Not for the meeting," Maria said. "You missed the meeting!"

"No, I didn't," I responded. Then I realized she wasn't talking about my playground meeting with Ford. Maria didn't know anything about that. "Wait," I began. "What meeting?"

"I can't believe you forgot!" She huffed.

"Forgot what?" I asked. I thought hard, trying to remember what meeting I'd had with Maria.

"The Secret Pals Club meeting!" Maria said. "Thirty minutes before school in the library? We planned it last week. Don't you remember?" Maria had thought up a great idea for a club where the members would do secret, friendly things for people. She had thought it up as a way to be nice to people who didn't have many friends or who got picked on. She figured we could do things like notes and cards and stuff to cheer them up. It was a good idea, for reals, but I just had so much Wonder stuff on my mind that I had forgotten all about it.

"I'm sorry, Maria. I just had something else I had to do this morning. Something even more important."

"Like what?" Maria challenged. "What was more important than our new club?"

"She can't tell you," Ford said.

Maria made a little noise that sounded almost like a poodle bark. Her noise meant *How dare you!*

"Well, she can't," Ford told her. "That's just the way it is."

"She *can* tell me!" Maria argued. "Aleca tells me everything! Don't you, Aleca?"

"Sure," I said. "Mostly."

"Mostly!" Maria boomed. "But we're BFFs!" She looked at Ford and told him, "That means 'Best. Friends. FOREVER.'"

"I know what it means," said Ford, rolling his eyes. "But that doesn't mean she can tell you about *this*."

"Yes, she will!" Maria challenged. "Won't you, Aleca?"

Thank goodness the bell rang.

"We'll have to talk about this later," I

answered. "We don't want to be late!" I walked away and left Ford and Maria standing together with surprised looks on their faces. I just kept on walking, fast. You might even say running, because really, that was what I was doing. I was running away.

But I knew I couldn't run forever. Maria would want some answers, and she'd want them soon.

✳ 5 ✳

I Don't Think So Great
under Pressure

Mrs. Floberg had barely started her lesson on how to find the verb in a sentence when a little piece of balled-up paper landed on my desk.

I grabbed it quickly and held it in my lap so that Mrs. Floberg couldn't see me open it.

In pencil, in Maria's handwriting, the note said, *What is the big secret?*

I turned around and looked at Maria while Mrs. Floberg wrote on the board. I mouthed the word "NOTHING."

Pretty soon another piece of balled-up paper landed on my desk. *It's not nothing,* the note said. *What is the big secret? BFFs tell each other* everything*!*

Ugh! Little Ford and his big mouth!

What was I going to say? I thought for a few minutes and then wrote *It's personal* on the same piece of paper. I threw it back to Maria when I thought Mrs. Floberg wasn't looking.

I'd thought wrong. Mrs. Floberg *had* been looking.

"It appears that Aleca isn't very interested in finding the verb in our sentence," Mrs. Floberg mocked. She went to Maria's desk and snatched up the note.

Of course she read it out loud. Everyone giggled.

"Aleca, since you have wasted everyone's learning time, I think you should let us all in on your personal secret," Mrs. Floberg announced.

"No, thank you," I muttered.

"I wasn't asking if you'd like to," Mrs. Floberg said.

"Oh." I choked.

"Your secret, Aleca," said Mrs. Floberg. "You have exactly ten seconds to spit it out, or I'm sending you to the principal's office to share it with him personally."

The principal's office!

See, I really needed to *not* go to the principal's office. Because the principal and me, we had a history. A history of my unhooking his suspenders once when I stopped time, so that his pants fell down and the whole class saw his sailboat boxer shorts. Sure, he didn't know why his pants had fallen down, but he knew that I'd been in the room and had been about to get in trouble when it had happened. So probably he at least had it in his head that embarrassing moments and Aleca Zamm went together like ice cream and sprinkles. So probably he didn't like me very much.

"The secret?" Mrs. Floberg said. "Would you rather share it with us or with the principal?"

"I'd really rather not share it with anyone," I clarified. What was I going to do? Aunt Zephyr had said I couldn't tell anyone I was a Wonder. But I had to come up with something fast, something that sounded so personal that people would believe I hadn't wanted to tell even my BFF about it.

"It must be something really embarrassing," said Brett Lasseter.

Even though Brett is a toot and was just trying to make things worse, he gave me an idea.

I'd have to think up something awful. If it was embarrassing enough, Maria would stop asking questions, Mrs. Floberg wouldn't send me to the principal's office, and everybody would just leave me alone already!

I looked around the room quickly. I hoped maybe something would jump out at me. But all I saw were bright colors: the red bulletin board, the blue bookcase, the yellow baskets for art supplies.

Bright colors . . .

"My supersecret secret is," I began, "that my dad is a Whoop-Dee-Doo!"

✳ 6 ✳

Of All the Celebrities in the World, I Pick This One

As soon as I said it, I saw my mistake. Sure, now no one would suspect that I was a Wonder. But they would think my dad was a Whoop-Dee-Doo. That is, they would think it if I really, really sold it. So I said to myself, *Okay, Aleca! Start selling!*

"Your father is a what?" Mrs. Floberg asked.

"A Whoop-Dee-Doo," I said. "You know, that musical group that has the people in the weird costumes in all the bright colors? The group that has the TV program and tours around the country doing shows for preschoolers and kindergartners? I was never supposed to tell anyone, but my dad is one of them. He lives a secret double life."

"Your dad is a Whoop-Dee-Doo?" cried Joanie Buchanan. "Seriously?"

Everyone started giggling.

"Wait, which one is he?" questioned Scott Sharp.

"Oh." I grimaced. "I guess you would want to know that." I tried to remember the names of the Whoop-Dee-Doos. I hadn't thought about them much since I was in preschool. Back then everybody loved the Whoop-Dee-Doos. In fact, my mom had taken me and Maria and Madison to one of their concerts at the civic center.

"Yeah, Aleca, which one?" said Neal Martinez.

I tried to think of the names of the Whoop-Dee-Doos and blurted out the first one I could remember. "He's BeepBop-Boop," I declared.

"The blue one?" Brett Lasseter laughed. "The one with the boingy antenna things on his head and the giant squirty flower on his shirt? No way! That is so lame!"

"Yeah, well, you didn't think it was so lame back when you had the Whoop-Dee-Doos on your birthday cake and plates and balloons and everything!" I exclaimed.

Brett kept laughing. "But I was five!" he said.

He had a point.

"That is a total lie!" Madison shouted. "Aleca's dad sells medical equipment!"

"That's just the cover story we tell people to keep him in *cog-neat-o*," I insisted. "Cog-neat-o" is what famous people and spies get in when they don't want to be recognized. "He has to make people think he's just a regular salesman so he can keep all the little fans from mobbing him and stuff."

"Well, I can see why you wouldn't want to tell anybody *now*," Madison went on. "How embarrassing!"

On the one hand, I was glad that Madison had actually bought it and that, without meaning to, she was helping me sell it.

On the other hand, now everyone thought my dad was a Whoop-Dee-Doo.

And Madison was right—it was pretty embarrassing.

"Aleca's dad is a Whoop-Dee-Doo!" Brett repeated.

Of course the whole class burst out laughing. They pointed. They made faces.

Then, naturally, they all started singing the Whoop-Dee-Doos' theme song, which goes, "What will you do when the Whoop-Dee-Doos . . . open up their big bag . . . of fun?" Except that "fun" has, like, eighty syllables. When the kids in my class started singing it, they couldn't even get through the first few syllables of "fun" without practically dying laughing and having to start the whole thing over again.

I am not even gonna lie. It was humiliating.

"Oh, sure," I broke in as they kept singing. "Like you didn't think the Whoop-Dee-Doos were cool!"

"Not *now*," Brett taunted. "I mean, my mom bought me their potty training video when I was two, but—"

"I had that video too!" said his friend Braxton. "Aleca's dad teaches people how to poop!" They laughed and laughed.

"That's enough, boys and girls!" Mrs. Floberg burst out. It was almost like she was actually taking my side for once. But nobody listened. Everybody was talking or laughing. Mrs. Floberg had lost control of the class.

"That is the most embarrassing thing ever," Madison stated. "If my dad was a Whoop-Dee-Doo, I would take that secret to my grave!"

"I am almost embarrassed for her," Jordan said. "Except that it's Aleca, so who cares?"

So I'd convinced everyone. But now I was trying to think of a way out of it. I wanted to shout, *Scott Sharp picks his nose!* just to get everyone to laugh at someone besides me. But that would have been mean, and besides, everybody already knew that Scott Sharp picks his nose. And it wasn't Scott Sharp who'd gotten me into this mess. It was all me.

Maria asked, "Aleca, is your dad really a Whoop-Dee-Doo?"

"Of course he's a Whoop-Dee-Doo!" Brett cackled. "That explains why Aleca is such a dork. It's because her dad is a dork! He's the biggest goofball in town! He probably likes being a Whoop-Dee-Doo because the costume covers up that big bald spot on his head." He started singing the theme song again, and all his friends joined in.

Remember earlier that morning when I'd wished that I had said that Ford was Madison's mom's boyfriend? Because bringing somebody's mom or dad into it really ups the stakes?

Well, now Brett had done it. He had just upped the stakes. *A lot.* Braxton's crack about the poop had been one thing, but Brett had taken it to what you call a "whole 'nother level."

Brett and his friends could call me a dork all day long, but nobody was going to call my dad a dork! My dad could tell corny jokes with the best of them, but that is a dad's job. And sure, maybe my dad had a bald spot, but he couldn't help that. Plus, I happened to know that he was sensitive about it because he had special shampoo and also tried real hard to make the hair he did still have lie on top of that big shiny bald place.

My dad might have been corny and balding, but he was also good and smart and awesome. No way was I going to let Brett get away with saying mean things about my dad!

"Aleca Zamm!" I snarled. But nobody heard it over the song that Brett and his friends were singing.

❋ 7 ❋

Brett Lasseter Is Going to Get His One Day, but I Can't Wait That Long

It was nice how quiet it got all at once. Time stopping is a special kind of quiet. You don't hear the hum of the air conditioner or a breeze outdoors or even the flicker of the lightbulbs. It's 100 percent perfectly silent. And after all that mean laughing and singing, the silence was downright beautiful.

Mrs. Floberg had her top desk drawer open and was reaching for a coach's whistle. She does that when nobody pays attention to her. I think deep down she is probably jealous of our PE teacher because he gets to blow his whistle all day long whenever he feels like it.

Some of the kids were pointing at me. Some had their mouths open from singing that dumb song. Neal had sneaked out his phone and was trying to find the secret identities of the Whoop-Dee-Doos on the Internet. Good thing for me that the Whoop-Dee-Doos never told who they really were and that they wore those costumes that covered their whole faces. Nobody could prove a thing.

Maria's head was facing down. I went over and got a good look at her. A tear was hanging in the air between her head and her desk. I poked it because I like the way water feels gooeyish when time stops. Maria and I had been friends since preschool, and she had always been softhearted. I knew she was upset because she thought she had forced me to tell my big secret to the whole class. "It's okay, Maria," I said out loud. "I know you feel bad about all this, but it's not really your fault."

I sat on the edge of Maria's desk and thought. It was nice to have some quiet time to try to figure out how I was going to fix all this.

You know what would come in handy with a time-stopping ability? A memory-erasing ability. Or even a time-rewinding ability so you could fix your screwups. Too bad I didn't have one of those powers too.

Ford came into the room while I was

thinking. Oh, and I had started hula dancing too.

"What are you doing?" Ford asked.

"The hula," I clarified.

"Why?"

"Because I have a pact with myself that
whenever I stop time, I will do a dance. I try
to do a different dance each time. Today it
is the hula. Would you like me to teach you
how to do it?"

"I thought you weren't supposed to be
doing this!" Ford snapped.

"What, is there some law against the hula
that I don't know about?"

"Not the hula," Ford corrected me.
"Stopping time!"

"Oh, that," I said. "I had a good reason." I
explained everything to Ford. "So you see? I

couldn't let him say something mean about my own dad!"

"Children can be so cruel." Ford sighed. He sounded like a grown-up.

"Are you seeing anything?" I asked. "Any bridges or whatnot?"

"I didn't take the time to see if that bridge was there again," Ford explained. "I rushed right over to find you."

"Should we go look?"

"It's all the way on the other side of the school," Ford replied. "And isn't your aunt already going to kill you for stopping time? Do you think you should drag it out any longer than necessary?"

"The way I see it, I'm already in trouble," I said. "So why not make it count?"

"Well," Ford replied, "if you insist. Let's go."

"Wait a minute," I said. "Before we go looking for the bridge, do you see anything else?"

"Yes," Ford revealed. "There's a man standing by Brett. Or standing where Brett is standing. It's almost like they're standing in the same spot, overlapping each other."

"What does the man look like?" I asked.

"He looks like Brett," Ford responded. "Except much older."

"Hey!" I said. "Maybe you're seeing future Brett!"

Ford thought about it. "I think that's entirely possible," he guessed. "Assuming I saw future deejay and past Mrs. Young, this would indicate a pattern. Yes, this appears to be a future version of Brett. I wish I'd brought my notebook. We should record this data."

"Never mind the notebook right now. What does future Brett look like?" Boy, I wished I could see him!

"Rounder in the face," Ford said. He was squinting at Brett, like he was studying the overlapping man. "Wrinkled. Redder. Oh, and bald."

"Bald!" I replied. "Brett's going to go bald?"

"It would seem so."

"Yippee!" I yelled. I high-fived Ford. Well, first I put Ford's hand up to catch my high five. I think he'd never high-fived anyone before in his whole entire life, and I had to teach him how.

I was so excited that in the future Brett would be bald. He deserved it for making fun of my dad's bald spot. That is what you call "just desserts." I don't know why they call it that, because when I do bad things, I don't get a dessert.

"Is he bald all over or just in one spot?"

"All over," Ford informed me.

Ha-ha on you, Brett Lasseter! I said to myself, or maybe even out loud. *You're going to be bald when you get old! So there!*

Then I realized it would be years before Brett got old. That was a long time to wait, in my opinion. Brett needed some ha-ha on him right *now.* "Maybe I should go ahead and shave all his hair off," I told Ford. "Kind of jump-start things?"

"Aleca, don't be absurd," Ford said. He

sounded like a grown-up again. "For one thing, where are you going to get a razor? And the electrical current for clippers would be time-frozen anyway. Besides, isn't that a bit childish?"

Did someone say "childish"?

"Ford, you're a genius!" I said. "Wait right here!"

✳ 8 ✳

It's Not Stealing If It's for a Good Cause

I rushed down the hall to the pre-K classrooms, because to preschoolers the Whoop-Dee-Doos are still the coolest. "Sorry, kids," I offered, even though they were all frozen in time and couldn't hear me. "But I need to borrow a few things. I promise I'll return them later."

I rooted around in desks, backpacks, and lunch boxes. Then I returned to my classroom, where Ford was waiting.

"What did you do?" Ford demanded.

"I just borrowed some Whoop-Dee-Doos merchandise," I replied. "Don't worry. I'm going to return it."

Then I moved Brett's chair back far enough that I could stuff the things into his desk. "Let's see," I said, more to myself than to Ford. "Whoop-Dee-Doos fruit snacks? Check. Whoop-Dee-Doos pencil pouch? Check. Whoop-Dee-Doos markers? Check. And if this isn't the icing on the cake, then what is?" I showed Ford the small stuffed BeepBopBoop doll.

"How are you going to explain those getting into Brett's desk?" Ford asked.

"Easy," I answered. "By not explaining. Everyone will just assume they're in there because Brett put them there." For a smarty-pants, Ford needed a lot of simple concepts spelled out for him sometimes.

"But Brett will know he didn't put them there," Ford countered.

"Yeah, well, Brett can know the truth all day long. That doesn't mean anyone's going to believe him. And the more he insists that he's never seen these things before in his life, the less anyone's going to buy it. It's funny how that works out."

"Well, you still can't be too obvious," said Ford. "In fact, you shouldn't even be stopping time at all, and while we're talking about all this, time is staying stopped for a longer time. I guess. If there is a time when time is stopped. Which is a deep question. And anyway, I thought you wanted me to show you the bridge."

Ford was right, of course. I wasn't supposed to stop time, and I knew I'd better hurry up and finish my trick, especially if we were going to keep time stopped long enough to go investigate the bridge. It was kind of amazing that Aunt Zephyr hadn't already teleported to my classroom to let me have it. Maybe she was napping again and didn't even know. "I'll make this quick," I concluded. "Then we'll go check out the bridge."

"Aleca, you're not thinking this through," Ford said. "Brett is going to begin to suspect that something magical or mysterious is going on. You'll draw attention to the very problem you went to such lengths to cover up. Besides, is this really ethical?"

"Ethical?" I said. "Brett Lasseter doesn't

know the meaning of the word 'ethical'!" Neither did I, but from the way Ford had said it, I assumed it meant "doing the right thing." "You're talking about a kid who pours water on people's laps and then tells everyone they've wet their pants. You're talking about a kid who put a stick in Wilson Chicarello's wheelchair wheel last week during the bakery field trip so that Wilson would get stuck in the dough-mixing room. Do you know how traumatizing that is? Wilson can't even make a sandwich anymore without reliving that humiliation! And last but not least, this is the kid who, only moments ago, made fun of my very own dad, right to my face! I think Brett Lasseter's got it coming!"

"Very well," Ford sighed. "Get on with it, then."

I grinned at Ford because he saw my side of it now, and I made sure all the Whoop-Dee-Doos items were carefully tucked into Brett's desk. "All done!" I said. "Now let's go check out that bridge!"

✳ 9 ✳

The Most Majestic Bridge
I Never Saw

I followed Ford to the side of the school where the lunchroom was.

"East," Ford said.

"Huh?"

"We need to go to the east side," he replied.

"Which side is that? The right or the left of the lunchroom?"

"East," he said again, seeming sort of annoyed.

"Yeah, the thing is, I don't know what that means."

"Can't you read a map?" Ford asked.

"Well, sure, but I'm not on a map. On a map the east is on the right, but that is only if the map is right-side up."

Ford shook his head. "Just follow me." We rounded a corner, and Ford caught his breath. "Look! It's still there!" he gasped. "Oh, Aleca, isn't it . . . isn't it . . . majestic?"

"Umm . . . isn't what majestic?"

I didn't see anything except the Dumpster, which was definitely not majestic. Unless you count big green things with a horrible smell, rotten food smears, and a lot of flies as majestic. Which I do not.

"Don't you see it?" Ford insisted. "It's right here!" He pointed in front of him.

"Sorry, bud," I said. "I got nothing."

"You mean you really can't see it?"

"I mean I really can't see it," I replied. And in fact, I was wondering if Ford really could see it. Maybe he was imagining it.

Ford sat down on the ground, like he didn't have any breath. Like he was a deflated balloon. Like he had nothing left in him. "I can't believe you can't see it," he said. "It's so big. It's a bridge, after all. And such a lovely one."

I could tell he was really disappointed. "I'd like to see it," I said. "I just . . . can't."

Ford put his chin in his hand and made a thinking face. At least I figured it was a thinking face, but I suppose he could have just had a stomachache.

Then he snapped his fingers. "How

ridiculous of me!" He jumped up. "Of course you can't see the bridge! Why should you?"

"Well, bridges are kind of hard to miss, if they're actually there," I said.

"But you couldn't see the future deejay or the future Brett," Ford explained. "So why should you see a past bridge?"

Now I understood what he was getting at. "Right!" I said. "Seeing stuff out of their time is your thing, not mine. Duh! Why didn't I think of that?"

"Oh, I wish you could see it, though," Ford said.

"Why don't you try it out?"

"Try it out?"

"Yeah," I said. "Go for a walk on it. See how it feels."

"I can't just walk on a bridge that no one besides me can even see!"

"Well, can't you at least touch it? I mean, have you touched any of the things you've seen? Like, did you touch the old desk you saw in your classroom the first time I stopped time? Or did you touch young Mrs. Young when she was standing by old Mrs. Young? Or did you touch the future deejay?"

"I didn't," said Ford. "It never occurred to me."

"Well, now that it's occurring, how about giving it a try?" I suggested.

Ford put his hands under his upper arms. "I'm kind of scared."

"Come on. You don't have to walk across it. Just touch it."

"What if it . . . I don't know . . . zaps me into another dimension?"

"Oh, Ford, that's impossible," I said.

"So is stopping time."

The kid had a point. He was good at having points. "I'll hold your hand," I said. "If anything tries to zap you, I'll hang on extra tight. I promise."

Ford almost smiled. "I really would like to touch it," he said.

I held out my hand, and he took it.

We walked a few steps, and Ford slowly reached out his other hand. He let out a sort of "ahhh" sound. Not like, *Ahhh! A tornado is heading this way!* but like, *Ahhh! This is awesome.*

"I take it that you can feel it?" I asked.

"Yes," he said. "Here, you try too."

I put out my other hand, but I didn't feel anything.

"Remarkable," Ford said. "Your hand just went through."

"If you say so," I replied. "Do you want to try to walk across it?"

"I'd have to do it alone," Ford answered. "I'm not ready. Not today."

"You're probably right," I agreed. "We need to talk to Aunt Zephyr about this before we do anything else. This is a lot of new information."

For another few seconds Ford patted the bridge that only he could see and feel, and then we had to get back to my classroom so that I could get time started again. Aunt Zephyr wouldn't be napping forever.

✳ 10 ✳

Number One Fan

Once we got back to my classroom, I waited a little while after Ford left. When I felt sure he must have gotten back to his class, I said, "Aleca Zamm!"

Brett and his friends picked right back up with singing the Whoop-Dee-Doos theme song like nothing had happened. The only good thing about their obnoxious voices was that they took my mind off Ford's bridge and put it right back on getting even with Brett.

When they finished the song, I said very loudly, "That was great, Brett. But then, I guess you've had a lot of practice, since you're the Whoop-Dee-Doos' biggest fan!"

"Yeah, right," Brett challenged.

I looked at his friends. "If you don't believe me, just look in his desk."

They stood there a moment and then bent down to dig in Brett's desk.

"There's nothing in there," Brett insisted. "Hey, what're you doing?" They kind of shoved him out of the way and went right on digging.

"Look!" said Tate. "Whoop-Dee-Doos fruit snacks!" The class gasped.

"Man, Brett!" yelled Braxton. "What're you doing with a Whoop-Dee-Doos pencil case and markers?"

71

"Forget the pencils and markers," Tate chimed in. "He's got a doll!" He held up the stuffed BeepBopBoop.

It was pretty funny the way everyone moved quickly away from Brett. It was like they thought that liking the Whoop-Dee-Doos in fourth grade was contagious. I mean, no kidding—you'd have thought Brett had lice. Lice that would also throw up all over you! Lice that would throw up all over you and then make you eat fish eyeballs!

"Those are not mine!" Brett yelled. "It's a trick!"

But no one was listening. They were laughing too hard.

Mrs. Floberg blew her coach whistle. I bet she was glad she got to do that. The class grew silent. "That is ENOUGH!" she said.

"But I can explain . . . ," Brett began. Mrs. Floberg stood there, and we all waited. But Brett didn't explain anything, because how could he?

Once class started again, I whispered "Aleca Zamm" and stopped time once more so that I could put the Whoop-Dee-Doos merchandise where it belonged. I didn't want the kid who had the BeepBopBoop doll to start crying or anything.

I was very quick about it so that maybe Aunt Zephyr would be less mad. I did a fast disco dance I'd seen on the Internet, where you just point your finger up and down a few times and that is considered a dance. Then I ran down the hallway to the pre-K rooms. I had to pass Ford's classroom on the way.

"Not again!" he called when he heard me run past.

"Don't judge me!" I called back. And I kept on running.

✳ 11 ✳

I'm Pretty Sure Everyone Secretly Still Likes the Whoop-Dee-Doos

Once I started time again, Brett faked a stomachache so that he could go to the office and call his mom to take him home. What a big baby! He is such a baby that he *should* still watch the Whoop-Dee-Doos. At least when I told everyone that my dad was BeepBopBoop, I stayed at school and took it like a boss.

The funny thing was, now that everybody thought Brett was a secret Whoop-Dee-Doos superfan, nobody seemed to think it was that bad that my dad was supposedly one of them. Madison and Jordan still sneered and giggled at me during lunch, but a few kids in my class actually seemed kind of starstruck and wanted to know if my dad knew any other people who were legit famous without dancing around in goofy costumes. They'd say, "Does your dad know . . ." and then name somebody famous. I would say no, but no one would believe me. They would just think I was being modest or that I wasn't supposed to tell. The more I denied that my dad hung with celebrities, the more everyone wanted to believe he actually did. Kind of like how the more Brett denied liking the Whoop-Dee-Doos, the less everyone believed him. People are funny that way.

I guess the whole Whoop-Dee-Doos thing didn't really end up being so awful after all. And the best part was, Maria wasn't mad anymore. In fact, she was the opposite of mad.

"Oh, Aleca, how can you ever forgive me?" she asked at lunch. "I'm a terrible friend!"

It made me feel guilty, so I told her, "No, you aren't."

And then she continued, "Yes, I am! If it weren't for me, you never would have had to tell your embarrassing secret!"

Well, she had a point. All of this *had* kind of been her fault. But on the other hand, I had kept something important from her *and* I had accidentally ditched her club meeting. But just to make Maria feel better, I let her give me half of the homemade churro her mom had put in her lunch, and then we called it even.

"Isn't that strange, about Brett loving the Whoop-Dee-Doos? At our age?" Maria asked.

"Strange," I said.

"And what was he thinking, keeping those things in his desk? It's almost like he *wanted* to get caught!"

"You're right," I replied.

"It's all so strange that it's almost like . . . like . . . magic!" Maria theorized.

"There's no such thing as magic," I said, maybe too quickly.

"I don't know," Maria said. "It's so odd, the way he got caught right when he was making fun of you about it. It's almost like something happened . . . or somebody did something. . . . I don't know. All I'm saying is that if I were magic, I would have magically put all that stuff in Brett's desk right then, at that very moment."

"No, you wouldn't." I smiled. "Even if you could, you're too nice to even think about doing something like that. It wouldn't be like you at all."

Maria laughed. "Yeah, maybe you're right," she decided. "It doesn't sound like me." She paused. Then her eyes got kind of big. "It doesn't sound like *me*, Aleca. It sounds more like . . . well, like *you*."

Now I laughed. The nervous kind of laugh.

"Aleca . . . Did you . . . Do you . . ."

I laughed again, trying to sound less nervous this time. "Do I have magic powers to make people suddenly have

Whoop-Dee-Doos pencil pouches in their desk?"

Now Maria saw how silly it sounded. She really started laughing. "Wouldn't it be fun if you did?" Then she stopped laughing. "So, I mean . . . do you . . . I mean . . . is it . . ."

Maria couldn't find the words to say what she wanted to say. So I tried to help her out. "What is it, Maria? Don't worry. You can ask me anything."

Maria blushed. "I just . . . I mean . . . is your dad really BeepBopBoop? I find it kind of hard to believe that for all the times I've been to your house, I never once had any clue."

I didn't want to lie directly to Maria, because she was my friend. So I asked, "Why would I make up something like that?"

Maria looked at me like she was studying me. Kind of the way Ford had that morning, when he'd been trying to figure out if I was superbrave or just didn't have common sense. (Come to think of it, he never did tell me what he decided about that.)

"What is it?" I asked Maria.

"I don't believe you," she said. "I'm sorry, Aleca, but I know you. And I know you're hiding something from me."

Uh-oh! "You do?" I asked.

"Yes," she proclaimed. "And I know what it is."

I gulped. And this time I asked even more nervously, "You do?"

"Your dad isn't a Whoop-Dee-Doo," Maria said. "I know why you said he is, though. It all makes sense now."

I didn't say anything back. I didn't know what to say.

"Aleca, I know your secret. And I know why you didn't want to tell me."

Suddenly I got this great feeling. Because Maria knew! I had kept my promise to Aunt Zephyr about not telling Maria that I was a Wonder, but Maria had figured it out on her own! And now life would be so much easier and so much less stressful because Maria knew everything and we could talk about it and not have this big giant secret between us. But I wouldn't get in trouble for telling her! Of course, I'd have to swear her to secrecy. And knowing how Maria couldn't keep a secret, that was going to be hard, but still.

"You really know?" I asked.

"It's so obvious!" Maria replied.

"And you understand why I couldn't tell you?"

"Absolutely! You were too modest to tell me the truth. And also, you wanted to protect Ford."

"Well, it wasn't really modesty," I said. "I mean, I totally wanted to tell you, but . . ." Then I wondered, *Wow! How does she know about Ford, too?* That girl was *good*!

"You're so wonderful, Aleca," Maria reassured me. "And I'm sorry that I got angry with you about missing the meeting. You hadn't forgotten about the Secret Pals Club at all—you were already starting it!"

Suddenly I got the idea that maybe Maria and I weren't talking about the same thing. "I was?" I asked.

"Of course," she replied. "You missed the meeting because you were being a pal to Ford, because you could tell when we saw him at the skating rink how much he needed a friend. That's why you met with him this morning. But you didn't want to embarrass him by telling me you were helping him or make him feel like you were just being his friend because you felt sorry for him. And then I pushed and pushed, and you came up with that wacky Whoop-Dee-Doos story just to protect Ford and to keep from bragging about your good deed. You took public humiliation instead! That is so amazing of you!"

"Oh." I grimaced. Well, now I had to roll with it. "So I guess you figured it all out, then." I felt kind of sad that Maria had it all wrong. Because not only did I still have to keep my real secret from her, but she was also giving me credit for being a lot nicer than I actually was. Which made me feel guilty.

"That was so nice of you to reach out to Ford," Maria said.

"Don't give me too much credit, Maria," I cautioned. "I'm not exactly doing Ford any favors. I like him. He's very interesting. And he's a nice kid."

Once I said it out loud, I realized I meant it.

✳12✳

Aunt Zephyr's Wonky
Wonder-ing

I'd sort of solved my problems at school, but when I left to go home, other problems were just beginning.

As it turned out, Aunt Zephyr had not been napping while I'd been at school, and she knew all about how I'd stopped time to get revenge on Brett. She knew, and she was not happy.

She was in the car with Mom at pickup time. Mom asked, "What'd you do at school today, sweetie?" and Aunt Zephyr said, "Yes, do tell."

So I had no choice but to spill it—*all* of it. Except for the part about Ford, because Aunt Zephyr and I had kind of not mentioned to Mom and Dad that there was another Wonder in town. It wasn't that we were trying to keep secrets from them. But Aunt Zephyr felt that Mom was about two more shocks away from a nervous breakdown, so we were trying to freak her out as little as possible. Or at least freak her out in small doses. Even without the Ford part of the story, Mom got all upset and nervous again. Mainly because of the time-stopping thing, but also I think because she was kind of embarrassed for people to think her husband was a Whoop-Dee-Doo.

"Aleca, you were expressly forbidden to stop time again!" Mom said.

"But I had to defend Dad's honor!" I protested.

"Aunt Zephyr, why didn't you just teleport to the school and make her behave?" Mom asked.

"I can't time-police her forever, Harmony," Aunt Zephyr announced. "She's got to learn some self-control on her own."

But when we got home, I found out that that wasn't the real reason.

Mom dropped us off and went to pick up Dylan. She wanted Aunt Zephyr to have time alone with me so that Aunt Zephyr could really give me the business, I guess.

"I wish you *had* showed up at school when I stopped time," I told her. "Something happened that I've been dying to tell you about. Ford saw this bridge. And he took me to see it, but I *couldn't* see it. So I talked him into touching it, and he did. But when I tried to touch it too, all I felt was air."

"I wish I had been there too," Aunt Zephyr said.

She didn't sound all that excited about the bridge thing, though. Instead she sounded sort of quiet and frightened.

"If you knew I'd stopped time again," I said, "why didn't you just teleport to my classroom?"

"Not for lack of trying, I'm afraid," Aunt Zephyr claimed.

"You mean you tried but you couldn't get there?"

"Yes," Aunt Zephyr replied. "I concentrated very hard. I just couldn't do it."

"So all that stuff you said in the car, about not policing me—"

"A cover-up. I was trying not to burden your mother. I didn't want her to know of my failure."

"Did you think yourself somewhere that you didn't intend to go?" I asked. "Is that what happened?"

"No. Worse than that. I stayed put. I didn't move an inch." Aunt Zephyr sat on the bed and put her head in her hands. "I've lost it, Aleca. It's all gone."

I sat down beside Aunt Zephyr and patted her. I mumbled, "There, there," like I've seen people do on TV when someone is upset.

"Maybe you ought to try again?" I said.

"Oh, what's the use?"

"Well, the use is not giving up so easily. Just because you couldn't do it today doesn't mean you can't ever do it again."

"Hmmm," Aunt Zephyr conceded. "I hadn't thought of it like that. I guess I was throwing a pity party a bit prematurely."

"I'm sure you just had an off day," I suggested. "You can try again tomorrow."

"Tomorrow?" she scoffed. "Haven't you ever heard the expression 'There's no time like the present'? You wait here. I'm going to take a quick jaunt to Riviera Maya. It's a gorgeous spot on the Caribbean coast." She opened up the closet and pulled out a big floppy hat and some sunglasses. "Here goes nothing," she said.

I watched while Aunt Zephyr took a deep breath and closed her eyes.

Then I heard the door open downstairs. "Aleca?" my mom called.

"I'll be right back," I promised Aunt Zephyr.

I went downstairs and answered Mom's questions about my homework, what I wanted in my lunch for the next day, and whether I thought I ought to wash my hair again that night even though I had just washed it the night before.

Then I ran back upstairs to check on Aunt Zephyr.

Good news! She was gone.

✳ 13 ✳

Someone Is on Our Roof, and It Isn't Santa

I expected Aunt Zephyr to come right back. Exactly how long was a "quick jaunt" anyway? I wasn't sure. But at least ten minutes, maybe twenty, had passed, and Aunt Zephyr hadn't returned.

The phone rang. We were one of the last families on earth to have a landline, so I yelled, "I'll get it!"

I didn't recognize the number, but I answered right away. "Hello?"

"Aleca, it is I," said Aunt Zephyr. I thought I heard country music playing faintly in the background.

"Thank goodness!" I whispered so Mom couldn't hear. "How's Riviera Maya?"

"Not at all like I remembered it," Aunt Zephyr complained.

"It's not?" I asked.

"I'm nowhere near Riviera Maya," Aunt Zephyr said. "From the best I can tell, I am currently in an extremely small town in Wyoming."

"Wyoming!" I squeaked. "What'd you go there for?"

"Chalk it up to bad aim," Aunt Zephyr speculated. "I told you my ability was on the fritz. When I opened my eyes, here I was, in the middle of nowhere, standing on the side of a highway. A truck driver gave me a lift. I'm at a trading post of sorts."

"When are you coming home?"

"I'm not sure," she lamented. "I'll keep trying to concentrate. Don't say anything to your parents yet."

After we hung up, I went downstairs to help Mom make tacos for dinner. I tried to act like nothing was wrong. Mom didn't ask what Aunt Zephyr was doing or anything, so I guess she thought Aunt Zephyr was upstairs because she was bunking with me during her visit.

Dad came in from work. He kissed my mom on the cheek and said, "How was your day?"

"Fine," my mom replied. "By the way, if anyone asks, you're secretly a Whoop-Dee-Doo."

"A what?" he asked. Before Mom could explain, we heard a loud noise on the roof. Dylan came running downstairs.

"What in the world was that?" Mom shouted.

Dad looked at me. "Where's your great-aunt?"

But he didn't wait for me to answer. Instead he went running outside. Mom, Dylan, and I followed.

"Aunt Zephyr!" Dad yelled. "Are you all right?"

Aunt Zephyr was lying on her stomach on the part of the roof that juts out past my window.

"What in the world are you doing on the roof?" Mom called.

"Just help me down," Aunt Zephyr replied.

Once Dad got the ladder and carefully helped Aunt Zephyr to the ground, Mom scolded her. "You could've fallen off and gotten hurt!"

"What were you even on the roof *for*?" Dylan asked.

Aunt Zephyr looked at me like she could use a little help. I had to think fast. "Were you trying to get a tan?" I asked. (Notice I didn't lie; I just asked a question.)

"A suntan . . . yes! A suntan!" Aunt Zephyr answered. "My foolish vanity got the better of me." She gave me a wink that nobody else saw. "The roof seemed like a good place to catch a few rays."

"Aunt Zephyr, I'm surprised at you," said Mom. "Endangering yourself to get a suntan?"

"Yeah. That's, like, totally bad for your skin," said Dylan.

"And for breaking your neck," added Mom, "which could have easily happened! Honestly, Aunt Zephyr, can't I leave you alone for one minute without your courting mischief?"

"A little mischief keeps life interesting, Harmony," she replied, patting Mom's shoulder. "You ought to try it sometime."

Mom shook her head and went back into the house. Dad and Dylan followed her.

Once they were gone, I told Aunt Zephyr, "Hey, at least you made it back here, even if you did land on the roof."

"Yes, at least," she said. "Although there were a few detours between here and Wyoming."

"Detours?"

"From Wyoming, I teleported to the middle of a vineyard in Sonoma. From there I wound up in Cancún, and I don't mind telling you, I was pretty tempted to stay put, after the day I've had. But nevertheless I tried again. Only this time I landed in Barcelona."

"I guess we'll have to keep working on things," I said. "In the meantime, what about Ford's bridge? Isn't there some kind of way that you and I could see it too?"

"I'm in no frame of mind right now to even think about Ford's bridge."

"How can you say that? This is the opportunity of a lifetime!"

"I doubt that," Aunt Zephyr said. "I doubt I will ever be able to see that bridge. After all,

I was never able to hear the animals talk to my brother Alec. It all just sounded like animal noises to me. And I certainly couldn't hear people's thoughts when Zander read minds."

"And I guess you couldn't take either of them with you on your trips?" I asked.

Aunt Zephyr cocked her head to the side the way dogs do when you make a weird noise. "You know, come to think of it, I never even tried."

"Ooh! Ooh!" I exclaimed. "Try now! Take me!"

"I don't think that would be the wisest course of action, given my difficulties of late. Suppose I were able to take you with me somewhere, and then we couldn't get back? Your mother would blow a gasket."

Even though I didn't know what gaskets were and how they blew up, I figured Aunt Zephyr was probably right.

"Can we try tomorrow?" I asked. "When you're all rested up?"

"We'll see," Aunt Zephyr said. "To tell you the truth, Aleca, I wouldn't mind seeing Ford's bridge myself, if we can find a way."

✳ 14 ✳

I've Never Been This Excited about Research in My Whole Life

The next day, though, Aunt Zephyr wasn't in the mood to try teleporting me or seeing Ford's bridge. Unfortunately, she was still down in the dumps about accidentally winding up in Wyoming and then landing on the roof when she got back.

"Do you want to meet me and Ford after school?" I asked her that morning. "Or really, during school, if you want. I could stop time whenever, and we could give it a go about seeing his bridge and finding out what's on the other side."

"I don't think so, Aleca. It's probably for the best if I don't take any unnecessary risks," she replied. "I'll be lucky if I can hang on to the shred of my ability that I still have. I can't try to tack on anything else! And besides, you're not supposed to be stopping time, remember?"

"But this wouldn't be stopping time just to do it," I said. "It would be for . . . research!"

"No research for me, thanks," said Aunt Zephyr. I think she meant it to be sort of funny, like she was turning down a slice of pie. But I couldn't help noticing that she'd said, *No research FOR ME.* Which was almost permission for Ford and me to do research FOR US. I doubted that was what she actually meant, but I figured I could still make a good case for misunderstanding her later when I got in trouble for what I was pretty sure I was about to do.

As eager as I was to see Ford, I was still kind of nervous about going to school that day, seeing as how everyone thought my dad was a Whoop-Dee-Doo. Turns out I worried for nothing. Maria met me at the door. She was wearing sunglasses, which was not something she usually did. She was also wearing a big grin.

"What's with the shades?" I asked.

"Don't worry. I brought some for you, too." She handed me an oversize pair.

I put them on. "What are these for?"

"If your dad's a celebrity, then that makes you a celebrity. And as your bestie, that makes me a celebrity."

"But I already told you, my dad's not really BeepBopBoop," I whispered.

"I know that, and you know that." Maria grinned and gestured to a group of kindergartners behind her. "But they don't know that."

We tried not to giggle as we walked past them like we were movie stars on a red carpet. The kindergartners whispered and pointed, but they were too intimidated to talk to us. After all, I was practically a legend in their eyes: BeepBopBoop's daughter, at their own school. Some of them took pictures of Maria and me with their phones as we walked past. I tried not to think about the fact that even some kindergartners had phones and I still didn't.

Maria and I took off our shades before

we got into Mrs. Floberg's room. Being BeepBopBoop's daughter (supposedly) didn't make me cool to fourth graders, but at least I wasn't hassled. No one in my class wanted to tease me about it anymore because Brett had threatened to give a real beat-down to the first person who breathed a word about the Whoop-Dee-Doos ever again. And for the rest of the day, if anyone so much as looked at him, Brett said, "What're you looking at?" So nobody—not even Madison or Jordan—said anything to me or anyone else about the Whoop-Dee-Doos.

I was glad that the whole thing had blown over, because I had bigger fish to fry. And by "fish" I mean Ford, although I wasn't going to fry him, just talk to him.

But it is actually pretty hard for a fourth

grader to get a little time with a third grader, because our grades never did anything on the same schedule. We ate lunch at different times, and we went to the playground at different times. This meant that if I wanted to talk to Ford, I was going to have to be sneaky. So that is why when I saw Ford's class pass by our door on their way to the playground, I started coughing.

Cough, cough, cough. Mrs. Floberg looked up from her desk. We were all supposed to be in silent work time. When I stopped coughing, she looked back down. Then I did it again. *Cough, cough, cough.* She looked up again, then back down again. *Cough, cough, cough,* I did again, but this time I added a really big *blech* onto the end, like I was going to cough up a lizard that was stuck in my throat. It was the grossest *blech* I'd ever heard, and I felt proud. But I remembered not to smile, because no one smiles when they are coughing up a lizard.

"Aleca!" Mrs. Floberg barked. "Must you disrupt the entire class? Go get a drink of water from the fountain."

I coughed a few more times to really sell it, and then I was out the door. I even coughed as I was walking out. I was good.

I saw Ford at the end of the line. I grabbed his arm and pulled. "Hey!" he whimpered.

"Shhh!" I said. "Come with me!"

"I can't," he cried. "I'll get in trouble."

"Oh, fladoodlecakes!" I told him. "Come on!"

I pulled Ford into the empty choir classroom. "Listen up," I said. "We've got to do

108

some research." I told him all about Aunt Zephyr's wonky Wonder-ing and how she was in no mood to help us with the bridge project. "But she didn't exactly say we couldn't try to figure it out ourselves."

"A loophole," Ford said. "It might be unwise."

"It also might be awesome," I suggested.

"Very well. When do you want to do this research?"

"Why not right now?"

"Has anyone ever told you that you're extremely impatient?"

"Yes," I said. "But can we talk about that later? I want to stop time right now."

"Okay," Ford sighed. "Go ahead."

I was so excited, I could hardly keep from yelling . . . "Aleca Zamm!"

✳ 15 ✳

"Walking on Air" Isn't Just an Expression

You might think that stopping time would get old after you've done it a few times.

But you'd be wrong. Stopping time never gets old. It is the coolest. Every time, there is something new and interesting to see.

Like on this particular day, a kid in the hallway had sneezed just a half second before I'd said my name. And so his little snot particles were just sitting there in the air. It was very educational. And gross, of course—but mostly educational. Because, you know how they tell you to sneeze into your elbow because your sneeze germs go everywhere? Well, they aren't kidding. That kid had a trail of yuck all the way to the other side of the hallway. "I am not walking through that!" I told Ford. We went around the other side, because otherwise it would have been like walking through a snot spiderweb, which would have been not at all pleasant.

Also, in another classroom we passed on our way outside, there was a boy who had fallen asleep at his desk, and three other boys were crowded around him, smiling. It looked to me like they were going to do something to the sleeping boy to embarrass him. So I sat him up in his desk and pulled his eyes open, because when time started again, the other boys would think the sleeping boy had suddenly woken up, and then they would probably scream in terror and embarrass themselves instead of him.

"Friend of yours?" Ford asked.

"Never seen him before in my life," I replied.

"Then why are we taking time out of our mission?"

"As someone who can appreciate the beauty of an occasional nap at school, I just thought I should have his back." I patted the boy's shoulder. "Carry on, my good man."

"To the bridge," Ford reminded me.

When we got outside near the Dumpster, I asked Ford, "Is it still there?"

"Indeed it is," Ford said. "My, but it's a beauty. I do wish you could see it."

"And you don't see it when time isn't stopped, right?"

"Correct. I've tested that theory on several occasions now. I come here often to search for the bridge when time is passing. No bridge."

"Let's try to walk across it," I suggested.

"No way!" said Ford.

"Not by yourself," I clarified. "Both of us together."

"I doubt that will work. You can't even feel it when you reach out your hand."

"Well, we've got to try something," I said.

Ford sighed. "I suppose so." He reached out for my hand, and we took a few steps. "I can't believe it!" Ford exclaimed. "I'm actually walking on it! This is incredible!"

I hated to break it to him, but the only

thing I was walking across was a rotted-out stump. And from what I could tell, Ford was just stepping in dirt.

But then, a few steps later something changed.

I fell right into a hole. It wasn't a big one. It was like maybe where a small tree had been pulled up. Ford would have fallen too, but I guess he got distracted—and brave— because he let go of my hand and kept on walking.

Right across the air!

✳ 16 ✳

A Short Walk on a
Long Bridge

"Hey, Ford," I called, trying not to sound too urgent. I didn't want to freak him out while he was walking on a bridge that did not exist in our time period. "I don't mean to alarm you or anything, but maybe you could come back this way?"

Ford didn't seem to be listening. He was muttering words like "astonishing" and "remarkable."

"Hey, Ford," I repeated. "Why dontcha come on back this way now, okay?"

He turned around. "Aleca, what are you doing in that hole? Get back up on the bridge!"

"Yeah, that's just the thing. There is no bridge. Not for me, anyway. Which is why you probably need to come on back and let's do some figuring out."

Ford suddenly realized he was walking alone on his out-of-its-proper-time bridge. He gasped and ran back to me.

It was only a few steps, but a few steps in a situation like this one seemed to be a lot.

"This is the most incredible experience of my life," he said as he helped me out of the hole. "I don't know what to make of it."

"Me neither," I replied. "We've got to get Aunt Zephyr on the case."

"I'm surprised she didn't teleport here immediately when you stopped time," he said. "You're supposed to be in big trouble if you do that again."

"Yeah, well, like I told you, Aunt Zephyr isn't exactly teleporting up a storm these days," I said. "Did I mention that when she got back from Wyoming last night, she landed on our roof?"

"No," said Ford. "But that doesn't sound good."

"She's not in much of a mood to figure out Wonder stuff," I said. "She's all depressed."

"Well, if there's anything that should pull someone out of a depression, it must be something as exciting as this!" Ford suggested.

"Maybe you're right," I agreed. "Let's get back to where we're supposed to be. I'll start time again, and then when I get home, I'll fill Aunt Zephyr in on everything that happened here and see what she thinks."

"And I'll add all this to my data," Ford said. "I'll analyze it for any possible connections."

"You do that," I replied. Although, I didn't know what good any of that would do or what it even meant, really. But I hoped Ford did.

• • •

I let Ford catch up with his class at recess, and I went back inside. "Aleca Zamm!" I said. And just like that, time started right back up. I could hear the boys screaming in the room where I'd opened the sleeping boy's eyes real big. I felt good about that one. I walked into my classroom.

"Are you feeling better?" asked Mrs. Floberg.

"Better than what?" I replied. She looked at me funny, and then I remembered that I had made all those hacking noises so that I could be excused to the water fountain. "Oh, I mean, yes," I said. "I am feeling much, much better!"

And I really was, because when I got

home, I was going to get to fill Aunt Zephyr in on what had just happened with Ford's bridge.

I couldn't wait to see how excited she would be!

✳ 17 ✳

Saving Aunt Zephyr
from the Soaps

That afternoon when Mom picked me up at the car-pool area, Aunt Zephyr wasn't with her.

"Aleca, something seems very wrong with your great-aunt," Mom said, sounding worried. "Do you know anything about it?"

I played dumb. "What do you mean?"

"She seems . . . well, depressed. She just moped around the house all day. It's like the fire has gone out of her. Do you have any idea what might be the matter?"

"I can't think of any reason why Aunt Zephyr should be depressed," I answered. And see, I wasn't really lying. I said it really carefully so that it wouldn't be a lie, because my lying had been getting out of hand and I seriously needed to cut that out. And now that I had this new information to refresh Aunt Zephyr, I really did think there was no reason for Aunt Zephyr to be depressed. So I was technically telling the truth.

"Well, maybe you can do something to cheer her up," Mom said.

When we got home, I saw what Mom meant. "See what you can do," Mom whispered to me before leaving the room.

Aunt Zephyr was pretty much a wreck. She wasn't wearing any makeup. Her hair was a mess. And she was wearing her plaid bathrobe and house shoes. She was watching, of all things, a soap opera.

"Hi, Aunt Zephyr," I said.

She sort of grunted at me and kept her eyes glued to the television set.

"Aren't you going to lecture me for stopping time today?" I asked.

"Meh," she replied, shrugging.

Wow. This was serious.

I thought maybe I could ease her into a conversation. "What is that on TV?" I asked.

"*The Corrupt and the Reckless,*" she replied.

"Oh," I said. And then I guess maybe I didn't try easing into the conversation for long enough. I tried to start telling her about Ford and the bridge. She was not even interested. She shushed me so that she could hear the TV show's dialogue, which was not even worth hearing, if you want my opinion.

I decided to try to be patient and give it another couple of minutes. I sat down and watched a little bit of the show with her. A doctor and a nurse were in a surgery room. The doctor was pointing a gun at the nurse. He was mad because she wouldn't be his girlfriend.

"Aunt Zephyr," I tried again. But she shushed me once more.

Finally I couldn't help myself. "No offense, but this show is way dumb," I remarked. "Because if you want someone to love you back, probably pointing a gun at them is not the way to make that happen."

"Yes," Aunt Zephyr agreed. "But I just like watching people with bigger problems than mine. It gives me some perspective. At least no one's pointing a gun at me."

"And during surgery!" I continued. "That's got to break all kinds of doctoring laws."

"I'm sure," she replied.

"Aunt Zephyr," I said, "this isn't like you. You're not the kind of lady to watch people do dumb things on TV; you're the kind who is out doing them herself!" I thought about how that had come out. "I mean, not *dumb* things, but *things*," I reassured her. "Things that aren't dumb. Good things. Wonder-ful things! And, boy, do I have something wonderfully Wonder-ful to tell you about! Something exciting!"

"Oh, really?" She said it flatly, like she wasn't convinced.

"Yes!" I insisted. "Ford not only saw his bridge today. . . . He walked on it!"

Aunt Zephyr turned her face away from the television. I could almost see a tiny bit of that sparkle in her eye again. Then she said, "Tell me more."

I filled her in on everything that had happened.

"There's got to be a way that you and I can see that bridge!" I told her. "Isn't there anything we can do?"

"I wouldn't have the first idea how to go about it," she replied. "But I suppose we could make an attempt."

"Then what are we waiting for?" I exclaimed. "Let's attempt! Who knows what we might be able to do as Wonders if we put our minds to it? Can we please—pretty please with sugar on top—attempt?"

Aunt Zephyr grinned. "Little miss, I'm with you," she said. "Attempt we shall!"

Turn the page for a sneak
peek at Aleca's next
time-stopping adventure:

ALECA*ZAMM
Travels Through Time

The Importance of Proper Footwear for Invisible Bridges

I didn't see any good reason why we should wait until tomorrow to try to see Ford's bridge, but Aunt Zephyr saw three good reasons.

First, it was dark outside, and she figured that if we were going to try to make seven-year-old Ford walk across a bridge from the past—one that didn't exist anymore and that only he could see—we ought to wait until it was at least daytime to make it somewhat less scary for him. Second, she needed to rest up because her teleporting was way on the fritz and she'd had a hectic day of ending up in places she didn't intend to go. Third, none of us could drive to school. You'd think that a lady as old as my great aunt Zephyr would have a driver's license, but why drive when you can teleport? She'd never bothered to learn how to drive a car, so we needed to wait for Mom to take me to school the next day, since the bridge was just a few steps away from school.

I was so excited, I could hardly sleep the night before. The past few days—since I turned ten—had been pretty exciting. I had found out I could stop time just by saying my name, Aleca Zamm. That meant I was a Wonder, a person with a special, magical ability. Like my great aunt Zephyr and her brothers, who had also become Wonders when they turned ten. Before I knew I was a Wonder, I didn't think there was anything special about me at all. But now here I was, feeling very special, what with my ability to stop time, my teleporting great aunt, and my new friend who could see stuff from the past and the future. Like this bridge we were going to try to cross. That is not exactly something just anybody gets to do every day! I could hardly wait to get this day started!

But since we couldn't exactly depend on Aunt Zephyr to be able to teleport to school, we also had to come up with an excuse for why she'd be going with me. We decided we'd tell Mom that Aunt Zephyr was going to be giving a talk at my school about geography because she had been everywhere in the world at least twice.

"I suppose it should go without saying," my mom said when we told her the excuse the next morning. "But you won't be mentioning to the children that you teleported to these distant lands, will you?"

"Oh, Harmony!" Aunt Zephyr chuckled. "Sometimes we don't tell people the whole story for their own good. Don't you agree?"

Mom did agree. She just didn't know we hadn't told *her* the whole story. Because the whole story was that Aunt Zephyr would, technically, be lecturing the class about world geography, but nobody would hear it because time would be stopped and they'd all be frozen. But she would still give a short lecture, even if no one heard. That is what you call a loophole, and lately, I've learned how to find lots of those. When you stop time as much as I do, if you don't want to get in trouble, you have to know where to look for loopholes.

I did wish Aunt Zephyr had toned down her outfit, but Aunt Zephyr rarely toned down anything. Not her outfits, hairdos, or even the things she said. It was kind of embarrassing walking into school with her that morning. She was wearing a dress with multicolored sequins the size of pennies all over it. And as if the sequins weren't enough, the dress also had a lace collar and hem and big buttons down the front. She was also wearing a scarf in her hair, big hoop earrings, and high-heeled shoes with fringe that looked like fireworks exploding.

"Why is everyone staring at us?" she asked as we walked into the building.

"Because you are wearing every color of the rainbow and you are shiny," I replied.

"I will have you know that this dress is from one of the biggest designers in Italy," Aunt Zephyr said. "Obviously none of these children know fashion."

"Obviously they're only in pre-k through fifth grade," I said. "And obviously you are not in Italy but in Prophet's Porch, Texas. And obviously, it is eight o'clock in the morning and we are in a school. What did you expect?"

"Young lady, it is not every day that I attempt something as monumental as merging Wonder abilities. This occasion calls for something special!"

"You sure nailed 'special,'" I said. And I guess she had a point, even if everybody was looking at us like we were freaks. Because we were going to try to do something super amazing: tap into Ford's power.

See, whenever I stopped time, Ford could see things from the past and the future, and the last few times he'd seen this really cool old bridge. He could even touch it and walk on it. But he was scared to walk all the way across it by himself. I couldn't see the bridge at all, and when I'd tried to walk on it with him, I'd fallen. Not far, but still enough to know there was no bridge there for me. But Ford had kept on walking, and to me, it had looked like he was walking on air. I couldn't stand it. I had to walk on that bridge too, and see where it went. So we'd cooked up this plan with Aunt Zephyr to see if we could figure out how.

"Hi, Aleca. Hi, Ms. Zephyr." It was my best friend, Maria. She stayed kind of far from us and I didn't blame her. The last time she'd been around Aunt Zephyr, Aunt Zephyr had rubbed noses with her. It is a greeting in one of the countries Aunt Zephyr likes to teleport to. Maria had been pretty weirded out (you would be too if a complete stranger with orange-sherbet-colored hair suddenly stuck her nose on your nose).

"Hi, Maria," I said. "You're probably wondering what Aunt Zephyr is doing at school today." *Well, here we go again,* I thought. I was going to have to make up a story to tell Maria. I had been doing that a lot lately, and I felt bad about it. I couldn't tell Maria the truth, because Wonder-ing is super top secret. That is because Aunt Zephyr says that Duds (regular people) might be scared of Wonders, or that bad Duds might try to hurt us in some way. So we could not tell anyone. Especially not people who could not keep a secret, like Maria. Maria is the best friend I ever had, and I so wanted to tell her that I had magical powers and so did my aunt and my new friend Ford, but Aunt Zephyr had forbidden it. I had to keep making up reasons for the strange things that had been happening. Lucky for me that Maria was so sweet and didn't really have sneakiness radar. Otherwise she would have been hip to my scams.

"I *was* kind of wondering," Maria admitted. She was eyeing Aunt Zephyr's getup, and who could blame her? "Wow, don't those shoes hurt your feet?"

"Yes, they absolutely do!" Aunt Zephyr beamed. "And thank you for noticing! I do hate to suffer for fashion and not have anyone notice."

"Wait," I said. "You're suffering? On purpose? Why in the world would you do that?"

"Why, vanity, of course!" replied Aunt Zephyr. "What other reason could there be? My toes are crammed into these things like useless knowledge in the brain the night before a big test. And every so often, one of my calves has a muscle spasm that would knock a professional wrestler to his or her knees! But these shoes complete my outfit in the most spectacular of ways. Don't you agree?"

"I have some rain boots in my cubby if

you want to borrow them," Maria offered. I was just glad that the discussion of shoes had distracted Maria from her original question, about what Aunt Zephyr was doing at school.

"Here, Aunt Zephyr. Maybe you ought to have a seat on this bench and rest your calves and your crammed toes," I suggested. "Maria, I'll catch up with you in a minute."

Once Maria left and Aunt Zephyr hobbled over to the bench, I sat down beside her and whispered, "Your shoes really hurt that bad?"

"Terrifically," she replied.

"Aunt Zephyr, no offense, but what were you thinking?!"

"I already told you, I was thinking about how beautifully the fringe accents my dress!"

"No," I said. "I mean, did you really think

that this was the best day to wear uncomfort-able shoes? The whole purpose of bringing you to school was to see if we could walk across Ford's bridge. It would be hard to walk across a whole regular bridge in those things, but this is a magical bridge! Don't you think it would be best not to have to worry about uncomfortable feet at a time like this?"

"Hmmm," Aunt Zephyr pondered. "I guess it was pretty silly of me."

"I'll call Mom and ask her to bring your sneakers."

"Nonsense! I wouldn't dream of putting your mother to the trouble. Besides, she isn't at home anyway. Remember, she had to take Dylan to that doctor's appointment today?"

"Oh, yeah," I said. My older sister, Dylan, was having a wart removed. I guessed Mom wouldn't leave Dylan at the doctor just to go get Aunt Zephyr's sneakers. "I guess you could try Maria's rain boots."

"That was a nice gesture, but they'd never fit," Aunt Zephyr said. "Nothing to worry about, Aleca." She looked around to make sure no one was watching. "I'll just teleport home quickly and change shoes. I'll be back before you know it."

"But . . . ," I began. Before I could finish my thought, which was that Aunt Zephyr's teleporting was not very reliable lately, she was gone.

On the upside, her teleporting had worked immediately.

On the downside, there was no guarantee she'd teleported *home.*